FROM
GRASS
TO
GRACE

Julia Chinaeze Eto

Julia Chinaeze Eto

Email: juliachinaeze@gmail.com

Phone: 08023219360

First published 2021

ISBN 978 978 988 391 2

DEDICATION

For my late father, Leo Arimah Onyekwuo,
and
my mother, Josephine Nwanyaola Onyekwuo.

CHARACTERS

Ezinne, also called Nneoma or Nne by her mother

Mama Ezinne: Ezinne's mother (real name is Ugochi)

Chioma: Mama Ezinne's younger sister

Akunna: Chioma's friend, and supermarket owner

Elohor: Ezinne's friend at university

Uro: Junior's father

Junior: Uro's son

Akuudo: Uro's wife

ACT ONE

SCENE ONE

At home in their one-bedroom and sitting room house in Umuoma in Iriowe town, Mama Ezinne's only inheritance from her husband's family.

Mama Ezinne: *(soliloquizing)* Nne has taken time to come back today. It's already 7pm. I have told her repeatedly not to stay out beyond 6pm. What could be the matter now? Besides, I have warned her against going too far away from our neighbouring streets. Evil is around the corner these days, and I cannot stand any evil befalling her, my only child. *(She clutches her bosom.)* If it were not for her father's death, I wouldn't make her hawk in the streets. *(She is about to start her usual weeping, but she sights Ezinne, and her heart jumps back into its cage. She smiles and welcomes Ezinne.)* Nne m, *ezigbo m*, you are late today, and your mother is worried. *(She now notices Ezinne's worried and downcast look.)* Did anyone beat you, or have you lost some money? Come, my dear, come and tell me what happened. *(She hugs her.)*

Ezinne: *(mutters something and points down to the

lower part of her body)

Mama Ezinne: *Di m oo*! Has it happened again? I'm finished! Please come and tell me what happened.

Ezinne: *(sobbing quietly)* It's Junior. *(She sobs loudly now.)*

Mama Ezinne: Junior! Junior *Onye?* Uzo's son! Eeeh? *Efuola m oo!* That good-for-nothing boy. Eh? *Di m oo!* Come and see what Uzo's son has done to your only daughter. *(She continues to sob quietly, still holding on to Ezinne who is also sobbing. After a long sob, she quietly pulls Ezinne to the bedroom.)* Lie down so I can see what he has done to you. Did he get into you?

Ezinne: He tore my pants and pressed me down. His friend Udo wanted to hold me down for him, but I bit the two of them: Junior on his manhood, and Udo on his right hand. Blood gushed out, Mama, and they ran away crying. Junior said he would bring the police, Mama. That is why I'm so scared. He did not do it, Mama. That is my only happiness. He has been disturbing me for years now. Today, I was a few metres away from Ugwu Mgbako junction when he and his friend blocked my way. The street was lonely and I was already heading home because I knew it was time to go home. They delayed me, and even the few people that passed by did not know they were planning evil. When no one was in sight, they dragged me to that burnt shop by the corner of the junction. That was where he tried to do it. He had earlier told me we would die of abject poverty, and that selling bread would not give us a good meal in a day. He also told me he would have his way even if *Amadioha* appeared on the scene. Mama, I cannot say how I got the courage to bite the two of them. Will Junior die? I bit him at that wrong place, and he was bleeding. I don't want us to go to prison, Mama.

Mama Ezinne: Death is what he deserves, but I do not wish him dead. There are many wayward girls that will agree to his advances. He should go to them. Or did his troublesome father send him to you so that he would have the opportunity to deal with us? The old peacock - like father like son.

Ezinne: What does that mean, Mama?

Mama Ezinne: You have had enough trouble today, so I don't want to bother you with adult talk. But very soon, I will tell you. You are still too young, just fourteen years old. Go and have your bath. Supper is ready; I made your favourite *ukwa*.

SCENE TWO

Long after Ezinne has eaten supper, her mother lies in bed awake, as sleep has eluded her tonight, as she reflects on her life and that of her daughter.

Mama Ezinne: *(soliloquizing) Chi m oma, ekwela ka ihere mee m.* Only you know my struggles and my secret thoughts. You allowed me to lose my husband at the age of twenty-five, just six years after marriage. You allowed me to struggle alone until Nne was eight years old, old enough to help me hawk my bread, our only means of survival. She was only three when her father died. Now at fourteen, she is too tall for her age, beautiful and well mannered. Some of my friends are indicating their interest in her for their sons. But Lord, she has to go to school and break this cycle of poverty. *(She stops her thoughts abruptly as if to hear from God, but she hears only her daughter's voice.)*

Ezinne: Mama, do you sleep at all?

Mama Ezinne: Yes, my daughter.

Ezinne: Mama, if you did, you would not be able to answer my question. Please sleep. Everything will be all right. We shall survive. I will make you proud.

Just then, there is a knock on the door: Kpom! Kpom! Kpom!

Mama Ezinne: *(murmuring)* Who can it be - so late? I won't open the door now for any reason. It can be risky. *(The knock continues and later dies down – after some minutes.)*

Early the next morning, Mama Ezinne opens the door to find a letter on her doorstep – from Junior's father, warning her and her daughter to stay away from his son. If not, they would go to prison for assault.

Mama Ezinne: *(shouting)* He-goat! Animal! Let him come out openly, and I will disgrace him.

Ezinne: *(waking up)* Mama, what is the matter?

Mama Ezinne: It's Junior's father. He must have been the one knocking last night. *(She hisses.)* I picked this letter up from our doorstep this morning. He's threatening to imprison us. I am ready for him. Let him come, since he is shameless. You are growing up into a fine young woman, Nne, so I must tell you everything: Your father died when you were barely three years old. He was a great father and a loving husband. He loved you so much, but death snatched him away quickly. He was a civil servant - with the Ministry of Works and Housing. After his death, his brothers, led by Junior's father, took all he left for us, and I had to learn to struggle to put food on our table. Since his death, Junior's father has been making advances to me, threatening to deal with me if I continue to refuse his advances. Some men are terrible, but my daughter, be strong. Strength of character conquers all.

Ezinne: Mama, you have always told me my father was a good man, but why are other men bad? I hate him, Mother, and I pray God to punish Junior for me. Are you sure that not all men are like Junior, his father, and Mallam Dogo? I do not trust anyone of them. Let someone try me again; I will bite him to death.

Mama Ezinne: God will protect you, my daughter. You will not meet bad men in your life anymore. Some men are greedy and wayward. I want you to study hard, so you will be a great woman.

Ezinne: Mama, it will surely happen.

ACT TWO

SCENE ONE

Ezinne is in her house in Iriowe, preparing for the West African Senior School Certificate Examinations.

Mama Ezinne: *Nne*, please go and sleep a little. You sleep now. I will wake you up by 5.30am, so that you will be strong and healthy enough for your examinations. You have always done well in your studies, my daughter. You've always taken the first position in your class, from JSS 1 to SSS 3. You will be the best, my daughter.

Ezinne: Thank you, Mama. I have two papers to write on my first day. I cannot afford to sleep. I want to make As in all of them, by God's grace. I will sleep by 1am, and you'll help wake me up by 6am. Mama, my success will determine what we shall be in the future. Do not worry, I will not fall sick. Let me prepare in time, so that when I have any free time, I can help you hawk bread.

Mama Ezinne: *Nneoma*, God bless you, my daughter. You will pass your examinations with flying colours. My wish is that you will go higher in school than your father and I did. My parents did not have enough money to send me further than Senior Secondary 3, and so, here am I. Even though I do not have much money, you will go to university, my daughter.

Ezinne: Thank you, Mama. I will not disappoint you. I want to study law at the university.

Mama Ezinne: *(rubbing her hands together in an attitude of worship) Ekene dili Chukwu.* It is going to be so, my daughter.

SCENE TWO

Ezinne: *(arriving from school, excited)* Mama, my first two papers were good! I wrote well. I know the results will be great. Please pack some bread for me to sell tomorrow, when I come back from school.

Mama Ezinne: Praise God! *(She starts dancing, swinging her hips from left to right happily.)* I know He will do it; keep trusting Him. I have packed bread for you already. Sell what you can, my daughter, and come back home early.

Ezinne: Yes, Mama, I'll come back early.

Ezinne: *(in the street, the next day)* Bread! Bread! Come and buy fresh bread here. It's bromate free. *(She moves from shop to shop, as people interested in buying bread call her attention. Some young men in the street whistle as she passes by; she hisses and moves away from them, soliloquizing)* Thank God, sales are good today, and Mama will be very happy, and I will have money to pay for my send-off. As the head girl, I must be present for the occasion.

Mama Ezinne: *(later at home, exclaims excitedly)* Ah! My daughter, God always sends His angels your way to buy from you! Ten thousand naira within a short period! *(She starts dancing.)* Please go and have your bath, while I prepare your food before you start reading your books.

Ezinne: Thank you, Mama. I have already read for my remaining papers; it is just to revise them. Remember, I will finish the remaining papers next week. Please remember my plan to travel to Lagos after my examinations.

Mama Ezinne: OK, my daughter. Finish your examinations first. This Lagos of yours is not running away.

ACT THREE

SCENE ONE

Uro is in his sitting room, talking to himself aloud.

Uro: Proud woman, let me see who will save her. A church rat that doesn't know her condition. I will deal with her. I could have married her after her husband's death, but she refused. I've been waiting for ages now for her to come and apologize, but she has not done so.

Akuudo: *(coming in from the kitchen and interrupting)* Papa Junior! What is the matter with you? Has anyone died? Please tell me.

Uro: *(snapping)* Something more than death has happened. That arrogant Uzoma has insulted me again. And this time, I'll show her I'm a man.

Akuudo: Leave that woman alone! She has not done anything to you. He-goat! Shame! You are teaching your son to follow in your footsteps. I'll not be part of your schemes. The whole village already knows what your son has done. I've already ground the pepper I will put in his eyes. He-goats! *(She swiftly runs out of the sitting room.)*

Uro: *(getting up suddenly and clutching his wrapper in his hands, running after her)* Wait there and see what I'll do to you! How dare you talk nonsense? Just wait!

Akuudo: *(quickly runs into her room and locks the door, and from there shouts out)* Eh! Come and beat me for speaking the truth, my 'titled' husband!

Uro: *(fuming with rage)* Open the door and see what I'll do to you. I'll beat the hell out of you and send you back to your people for opening your mouth too wide. Go and tell her; she is your friend. I'll report her to the elders if I don't see her before the end of this week. Next week is the meeting of the titled elders. Then she will know I am a titled man.

Akuudo: *(laughing from inside the room)* Ha-ha-ha! Titled man indeed! You and your fellow titled men are birds of a feather: He-goats!

Uro: Open this door now or I'll break it. I built this house, not you. Come out and tell me to my face what you are murmuring about.

Akuudo: Everybody knows who you all are. Always running after widows and other women whose husbands are poor. *Ntoo*! This one has said no! Why don't you take her no, or you want to force her to accept you? Remove your eyes from what does not belong to you. Shameless 'titled' man!

Uro: *(still fuming)* I am still your husband! Open this door, and let me clip your mouth forever. I am still your husband.

SCENE TWO

At Mama Ezinne's house, late in the evening, Uro is seen at the door knocking gently but repeatedly.

Mama Ezinne: Who is that - so late?

Uro: *(whispering)* Come and open the door. It's I, Nze Uro.

Mama Ezinne: *(looking very frightened and confused, opens the door reluctantly)*

Uro: *(smiling pleasantly and touching her) Ezigbo! Ugomma! Nwaanyi oma*! How are you? *(Mama Ezinne keeps silent.)* I just remembered, I have not seen you for long and decided to come and say hello. *(Mama Ezinne still keeps silent.)* How is your daughter? I know that she must be sleeping now. I won't stay long. *(drawing closer to Mama Ezinne and trying to hold her hand)* Come let us talk in the basement. *(crooning) Nwaanyi oma,* you are looking more beautiful today.

Mama Ezinne: *(pushing his hand away impatiently)* Please tell me what you have come for! The sun has gone to sleep and I want to join it. Tomorrow is market day and I want to be up before cockcrow.

Uro: *(smiling sheepishly) Nwanyị ọma,* I … I hope you've considered my offer. You know I love you, and I want to take care of you and your daughter. I will open a shop for you, and you will not need to sell just bread anymore. I will …

Mama Ezinne: *(Stop!)* Please, I have told you no! Please go home to your wife. Open the shop for your wife! *Biko hapu m aka!* I don't want!

Uro: *(now fuming)* Do you know who I am? A titled man! I have the right to … to …

Mama Ezinne: My 'titled' in-law, please go home to your wife. (*slowly pushing him away*) Please go home! (She *quickly opens the door, shoves him out and bangs the door.*)

Uro: You will come crawling! (*fuming and talking louder*) I will make life difficult for you in this village. A titled man like me! Look at someone I want to help! You are not even as beautiful as my wife! Who do you even think you are? (*hisses, shakes his head and walks away angrily*)

ACT FOUR

SCENE ONE

Three months later, at Chioma's house, a two-bed-room apartment in Johnson Crescent, Yaba, Lagos State.

Chioma: Listen well, Ezinne. Lagos is vast. To a new-comer, it offers a lot of surprises, but be wise. I know you are very smart and you learn fast. Do not be a JJC ("Johnny Just Come"). If not, Lagosians will out-smart you. Learn your routes fast. I have discussed with Sister Akunna; she is very fond of me, and at-tends the same Church with me. She is a lecturer at the University of Lagos, and owns a supermarket not far from the house. Even though she is older than me, she is my friend. She is eager to meet you and wants you to start work as a salesgirl in her shop as quickly as possible. Hoodlums are everywhere; the roads are not safe at night. Stay away from men, and be home before 6.30pm.

Ezinne: Thank you, Aunty. I will work hard to save some money for my university education.

Chioma: *Ezigbo*, God be with you. Your intelligence will take you places, and my sister will come alive again. God will use you to elevate her. You are hard-working and intelligent; your mother has trained you well. My house has taken a new shape since you came. (*She looks around the house admiringly.*) It's now very neat and sparkling.

Please respect Sister Akunna. She is a very busy woman, but kindhearted. As you behave here, behave that way there too. Respect the customers; they are the reason the shop exists.

Ezinne: Thank you, Aunty Chioma. I have heard all you said. I will not disappoint you and Mama. I have my dreams and I want to live up to them.

SCENE TWO

Back in Iriowe, Mama Ezinne hears news of her daughter's progress.

Mama Ezinne: *(soliloquizing)* Thanks be to God. My good God, You have done it for me *o*! Since I heard the news of my daughter's results, I have been overjoyed. Five As and three Bs! I am overwhelmed. *(She kneels down and raises her two hands up in an act of thanksgiving.)*

Another good news: my daughter is now a Supervisor. Eh! Supervisor! *Chi m o!* I am the mother of a Supervisor! *(She stands up and starts dancing.)* Bad people wanted to spoil my daughter, but my prayers surpassed them. My daughter will go to university and marry a good man. Then, I will leave this place and my trade to babysit my grandchildren. Eh! *(She pauses her dance and stands akimbo.)* My daughter must surpass me!

Back in Lagos at Aunty Chioma's house, two months later.

Uchenna: Ezinne, come on. You are growing into a smashing beauty. I have been admiring you since you moved into our house. *(He advances close to Ezinne.)* Do not be shy, *Omalicha. (He tries to touch her hand.)* Your auntie is not at home yet. Let me tell you something before she comes home.

Ezinne: *(running away from him)* Please do not touch me.

Uchenna: *(rushes towards Ezinne and tries to rip her dress apart; a scuffle is heard in the background)*

Ezinne: *(pushes him away, screaming loudly as she rushes to open the sitting room door)* No! No! No! *(She bumps into Aunty Chioma.)*

Chioma: *(shocked and agitated)* Ezinne, ọọ gini? Why do you want to tear the house down**?**

Ezinne: *(catching her breath)* Aunty Chioma, welcome home. *(She looks over her shoulder at Uchenna.)* I just heard my mother is so sick and has not been able to sell her bread. *(She says this breathlessly, her heart pounding.)*

Chioma: Oh, my child! Is that why you want to bring down the roof! It's okay. I will call your mother now. *(She hugs Ezinne and sits heavily in one of the chairs, legs apart, rubbing her protruding stomach.)*

Uchenna: *(sits quietly in a corner, soliloquizing)* Thank God! God, please help me control myself. What would have happened to me if Chioma had caught me? Smart girl, I have always known she's smart. *(He shakes his head as if trying to come out of a trance. He now walks towards his wife.)* My sweetie, you are home early today. Welcome back.

Chioma: Thanks, dear. May the Lord be praised. I thought someone had died. *(to Ezinne)* Please calm down and come in with me. I'll call her now to confirm, and if it's true, I'll advise she should go to hospital immediately.

ACT FIVE

SCENE ONE

At the supermarket.

Ezinne: *(turning to Akunna)* Sister Akunna, many customers have today complained of our not having items like Green Tea and Coconut Bread. I told them we had them up to yesterday, and that we would soon have them again. They are really in great demand. I think we should stock them up in bigger quantities.

Akunna: You are right, my dear. I will do so. *(She pulls Ezinne to sit by her side.)* My child, I have made enquiries about your Part–time Studies. You are hardworking and intelligent, and I know you will succeed in life. *(She spreads her arms around the shop.)* See how you have helped me here, so that my sales have increased very much. I cannot thank you enough.

Ezinne: *(kneeling down)* Thank you, Ma. You have been kind and generous to me. I will not let you down. *(She lowers her voice and looks around.)* Please I would like to discuss something personal with you when you are free. Please do not later tell Aunty Chioma about our discussion.

Akunna: *(looking at Ezinne surprisingly)* I hope you are not pregnant!

Ezinne: *(stands up and exclaims)* Ah, ah! Sister Akunna, no ooo!

Akunna: Okay, my dear, later, before I leave today. *(She watches Ezinne admiringly and wonders what must be bothering her, soliloquizing.)* What can it be? I've noticed she's been withdrawn lately. Let me wait and see. *(She gets up to attend to a customer.)* Ehen, what do you want to buy please?

SCENE TWO

Ezinne in a serious discussion with Akunna in the inner part of the supermarket where the day's sales are calculated.

Ezinne: Sister Akunna, I have a big problem. *(She hesitates, looks at Akunna intently, then hesitates again.)*

Akunna: *(urging her on)* What's the problem, my dear?

Ezinne: It is about .... *Ndaa* Uchenna, Aunty Chioma's husband.

Akunna: Chioma's husband? What happened to him?

Ezinne: *(looking embarrassed)* He is trying to force himself on me.

Akunna: What! *(she exclaims with her hands on her head)* Why? Oh, my child! When did this happen?

Ezinne: Every time I go home early. That's why I prefer to go home very late in the evening, when Aunty Chioma must have come back. Please, Sister Akunna, *(she starts crying)* please, may I stay at the supermarket for a week? Aunty Chioma is travelling, and I'm afraid to be alone with *Ndaa* Uchenna.

Akunna: Do not worry. You can stay in my house. I will tell your aunty that I'm expecting some important visitors, and would require your assistance to entertain them. She already knows I'm alone in my house and can't prepare for the guests myself. My daughter who is outside the country, studying for her master's, would have been able to help me out, if she were at home.

Ezinne: *(drops immediately to her knees)* Thank you, Sister Akunna! God bless you.

ACT SIX

SCENE ONE

Chioma is seen packing her bags and getting ready for her trip.

Uchenna: Sweetie, this journey of yours is affecting me. I hope you are not going to stay too long. I'll really miss you.

Chioma: *(laughing)* I'm not going for a holiday. Mama is sick and wants to see me. You know my condition. I don't plan to stay long. Ezinne is here to help out with the cooking, but I've cooked enough soup and stew; so you are sure of your food. *(She laughs.)*

Uchenna: OK, Sweetie. *(He smiles as he begins to think aloud lustfully at the mention of Ezinne's name.)* Finally, I can be alone with Ezinne, my *Omalicha*! Thank God, the coast is going to be clear. It's this time or never. I'll be careful to cover my tracks very well. After this, we will continue secretly. That girl is tempting, with her wonderful figure-eight shape. She is like a model. *(At this thought, he smiles again.)*

Chioma's phone rings as she goes to the kitchen.

Akunna: Hello, Chioma!

[**Chioma**: Hello Sister Akunna! It's been quite some time.]

Akunna: Oh, yes! How are you?

[**Chioma**: I'm quite fine. And you?]

Akunna: I'm fine o!

[**Chioma**: Great!]

Akunna: How is the baby kicking?

[**Chioma**: Ha-ha-ha! Em.... We're doing well.]

Akunna: Good! 'Hope you're getting ready for your journey?

[**Chioma**: Oh, yes! You see, I can't wait to see Mama.]

Akunna: Sure! I hope and pray that she'll get very well soon.

[**Chioma**: Amen! Thanks very much, Sister Akunna.]

Akunna: Incidentally, I'm expecting some of my colleagues from the University of Ibadan. They'll be coming for a week-long Conference holding here.

I'd please like Ezinne to come and help me attend to them. She's very hardworking, and I think she can be of help, especially since I have no house help, and my daughter is no longer with me. I hope you will not tell me, No.

[**Chioma**: Of course, not! Ezinne'll certainly come over. I wish I could do more than this.]

Akunna: Oh, I'm really grateful to you! You have been such a wonderful friend.

[**Chioma**: Ah, please…. I'm sure that Uchenna can take care of himself when I'm gone. The food in the fridge will be okay for him until I'm back. I'll be travelling tomorrow, as I have told you.]

SCENE TWO

Three months later, at the University of Lagos, Nigeria.

Ezinne: *(soliloquizing)* God, you are indeed good. Look at me, Ezinne, at the university registering for my courses. A law student, a university Law student. I thank God for bringing Sister Akunna into my life, and for using her to save me from *Ndaa* Uchenna. And she has promised to talk to Aunty Chioma about my permanently moving into her house! God, I pray it works out perfectly, so that Aunty Chioma would not suspect anything; I wouldn't want to hurt her, and I wouldn't want to harm her marriage. *(She suddenly sights Elohor, and calls out:)* Elohor! Elohor!

Elohor: *(sights Ezinne and quickens her steps to meet her)* Oh, Ezinne! I have been looking everywhere for you. JJC, how far have you gone with your registration? I hope you're almost through, because I've come to take you to your Academic Adviser. He will explain to you all you need with your courses, and help you settle down to your studies.

Ezinne: Ah, that's very kind of you! I've since completed my registration. Thanks very much.

Elohor and Ezinne walk towards the Course Adviser's office, chatting excitedly, hands intertwined.

Elohor: *(pointing to a poster on the Registry billboard, and reading the message aloud)* This semester, Fechy Modelling Agency will be hosting the Freshers' Talent Hunt at the University of Lagos. *(She stops reading and exclaims:)* Wao! Pretty cool! *(She turns to Ezinne excitedly and explains:)* Once they pick a student, that student's life changes forever. Not only do they award scholarships, they also train one to be a supermodel!

Ezinne: *(shrugs her shoulders)* I'm not even interested in all that. I have to focus on my studies. You know, my course is a part-time one, and I have to work hard to help myself.

Elohor: You must apply. *(She playfully smacks Ezinne on her back.)* If not, I will apply for you. I wish I had your shape and beauty. I would be doing *iyanga*, eh! *(She begins to walk and move her head from side to side, mimicking a model's steps, but fails woefully.)*

ACT SEVEN

SCENE ONE

Akunna and Chioma are in the former's Supermarket.

Akunna: My sister, you are growing bigger and bigger every day. *(She looks steadily at Chioma's stomach.)* I hope you had a good trip.

Akunna: My sister, *(she laughs as she rubs her belly gently) thank* you *o*! Mama is much better now. In fact, I even suggested she should come to Lagos with me, but she refused. And thank you so much for Ezinne and her studies. She hardly sleeps at night; she is so serious with her studies.

Akunna: That is even why I want to see you. I want you to let Ezinne live with me for some time. Since I live in the University quarters, she doesn't need to go back home after lectures. You know, she closes late sometimes, and the roads are not safe.

You may discuss with her mum before I tell her myself. She is a good girl, and I want to help her achieve her dreams. You can also encourage her mum to come to stay with you when you give birth, so that she can be with Ezinne as well. They must have missed each other.

Chioma: My sister, thank you so much. I know you mean well for Ezinne. So let her stay with you, since it will help her study better. She can visit us on weekends.

Akunna: Thank you, Chioma. Take care of yourself, and do not forget to discuss with Ezinne's mother. Give my regards to Uchenna.

Chioma: Oh, I won't forget. I'll call her tonight. Thanks very much!

Akunna: See you at Bible Studies tonight.

Chioma: Sure! God bless you.

SCENE TWO

Three months later, at Akunna's residence at the University of Lagos, some noise can be heard from the outside.

Akunna: *(stands up in the middle of her sitting room, confusion lining her face)* What's happening at the gate? What is happening! I hope there is no riot. Eh, Ezinne is not home yet! These students! *(She rushes towards the door.)*

Ezinne: *(crying and shouting happily at the same time outside the gate, with other students)* Ma, *(she runs up and hugs Akunna)* they picked me! They picked me for the scholarship! *(Her fellow students pick up giving the good news:)* Ma, she is going abroad for a course! They picked her; she has got a full scholarship! *(Everyone of them seems to be talking at the same time.)*

Akunna: *(confused)* I do not understand. *(She shakes Ezinne.)* Scholarship! How? Where? *(She turns to the other students, waving her hands and screaming:)* Let her speak!

Ezinne: Sister Akunna, I applied for a scholarship to a Modelling Agency on Elohor's advice. I had refused to apply initially, but she went ahead and bought the form and filled it in on my behalf. When the Agency later invited candidates to the results' announcement event, Elohor and I went together, and I was picked as the winner. So, I am their 2020 Ambassador! I will be flown abroad for a three-month modelling course during the long vacation. In addition to the modelling training, I have been offered a free two-bedroom apartment, and a full scholarship to complete my studies.

Akunna: *(holding Ezinne's hand and happily dancing)* Really? I am so proud of you! Your mother will be so happy. Thank God! *(She waves her hands above her head, praising God.)*

Later in the evening, Akunna first calls Chioma, and later, Ezinne's mother, to relate to them the good fortune - a three-month modelling course, full university scholarship, and other great benefits. On receiving the news, Ezinne's mother is overjoyed.

Back in Ezinne's home town.

Mama Ezinne: *(praising God aloud and dancing)* My God has done it. He has turned me from a petty bread trader to the mother of a model and law student. He has crowned my hard work with huge blessings. *(A lot of people gather around in amazement as Mama Ezinne keeps on singing and dancing.)* My daughter is going places. Nneoma *m* is going abroad. I, a petty bread trader, now the mother of a Lawyer Model!

(All join in the dance, singing, even though, like Mama Ezinne, they don't understand what "Lawyer model" [the refrain of her song] means. All they know is that it is something great.)

Song

Ezinne - Lawyer Model

       Lawyer Model

       Lawyer Model

Ezinne - Lawyer Model

       Lawyer Model

Chi anyi oma - Lawyer Model

       Lawyer Model

       Lawyer Model

Ugochi - Lawyer model

       Lawyer Model

       Lawyer Model ....

They sing, clap and dance the usual Iriowe female dance steps - bending down and swinging their waists from side to side, in tandem with their feet.

THE END

GLOSSARY

Ugwu Mgbako: The village square where festivals are celebrated.

Ezigbo m: My good one.

Di m oo!: Oh, my husband!

Chi m o! Oh, my God!

Onye?: Who?

Amadioha: Igbo god of thunder.

Ekene dili Chukwu: Thanks be to God.

Omalicha/Omalicha m: The pretty one/My pretty one.

O'o gini?: What is it?

Ugomma!: (A beauty-praise name.)

Nwaanyi oma: A pretty woman.

Biko, hapu m aka: Please leave me alone.

Chi anyi oma: Our good God.

Nne oma m: My good mother.

Efuola m!: I'm lost!

Kpom! Kpom! Kpom!: Sound made, or words spoken by someone knocking on the door.

Ukwa: Breadfruit.

Ntoo!: Serves you right!

Ndaa: Younger people's respectful 'title' (in some Igbo areas) prefixed to an older person's name.

Iyanga or *Inyanga*: Pride, show-off.